Learning was never so much

fun !!

by Kieron Seamons

BAT

keep dreaming

'E' stands for Emily, that's me ! and I am on a mission to find the most wonderful animal in all of the world. Can you guess what today's dream animal is ?

If I had a dream I'd like to have a.......................

(Can you guess the animal ?)

'If I had a dream pet I'd like to have a bat. Hello little Bat' said Emily excitedly. Suddenly, a tiny Bat flies in around her. He is very happy to be Emily's dream pet.

'A bat is one of those very special creatures. It flies as you can see but doesn't look much like a bird at all, infact he looks more like a mouse . He has no beak like a bird and no feathers like a bird, but he does have these beautiful wings like a bird and a furry body like a mouse. Just like a very cute flying mouse.

'Some people say "blind as a bat", well that's not quite right.' Explains Emily. 'Bats can see very well in day light but Bats like to play mostly at night. Even we have difficulty seeing at night. They use sound waves to find food. The sound waves bounce back and it knows what the food is, so maybe that is why they have these big funny ears' She continued.

The bat is just as happy flying in the day light.

And in the dark too. Isn't that amazing !

'Did you know that Bats are mammals. They account for more than 25 percent of all the mammals on the earth! and Bats are the only mammals that can fly. They also eat a lot of bugs, so that will mean my house will be bug free.' Laughed Emily

Emily is very proud of her bat, infact the more she knows about him the more she loves him. 'well you must be a little tired after all that flying around, why don't you take a rest on this new perch I got you' said Emily. She puts him gently up on a wooden the perch.

The bat swings down and hangs by its feet. Emily looks at the Bat very confused. She put him back up but he swung down again. She tried many times but it continued to hang upside down. Emily knew a lot about bats but she didn't know that Bats always sleep upside down. She was very confused.

'Gasp ! My Bat is **BROKEN !!**' exclaimed Emily.

Emily was just about to take him back to the shop when she heard her friends coming ' You have a bat, Bats are in all my favourite movies. I want to take the movie star pet out for a picnic lunch !" Said Louie. Emily felt a little embarrassed but Louie could not wait to meet the Bat.

Finally, Emily showed them the Bat 'Sorry Louie, that won't be possible. The movie star pet is…………. broken!' said Emily sadly. Everyone looked at the Bat hanging upside down on the perch. Emily stands him up and then he swings back down. They all gasp in shock, this was a serious problem, but what could they do.

May looked at the poor Bat. 'Well I never have seen a problem quite like this but I have an idea' she said with a big smile. Suddenly, she he puts heavy goggles on, and raises a handful of tools and smiles.

May worked very hard. She was cutting, drilling a welding for a long time up till she stepped back and revealed a very strong metal perch.

'I think the wooden one was too wobbly, so my new and highly improved perch should keep him up perfectly.' said May. She was very proud of her amazing creation and the Bat seemed to like it very much too.

The bat flutters and fly around and the kids all watch with excitement, he makes his way over to the new extra strong perch, lands happily. Suddenly, the Bat swung down and was hanging upside down again. May was very shocked. 'The Bat must be broken because my new perch is solid' exclaimed May.

Emily and all the friends were very worried. The Bat was upside down again.

'Maybe, just maybe, WE are all upside down, and maybe last night the whole world turned upside down and we never noticed ! Everyone turns to Louie a little shocked. Louie is thinking hard for a moment, then smiles. 'I have an idea' excalimed Louie.

Louie's idea was that everyone should stand on their head, to make the Bat feel more at home. They all thought it was a great idea. 'You are a genius Louie!' Said Emily. 'who would have thought that the whole world would turn upside down over night! Now he looks great !'

Emily was very happy with the Bat now. 'Maybe we should put all the furniture back the right way too, before mum comes home, I wouldn't want her to worry and besides it would make the bat feel more at home.' Said Emily looking at the sofa. Well the kids thought this was a wonderful idea but the Bat did look a little confused.

Emily and her friends run around spreading glue on furniture and plants and everything is glued to the ceiling. They are very pleased with themselves. The bat is very happy to watch the children being so silly.

Just then Mum and Dad walk in to the living room and are very shocked to see furniture, TV and plants glued to the ceiling!! Emily and her friends are all standing very pleased with themselves. Mum screams at all the madness. 'We did it to make the Bat feel more at home, Mummy' said Emily with a smile.

Mum was very unhappy to see all her lovely furniture and ornaments glued to the ceiling and she ordered Emily to take the Bat back to the shop.

All the children and the Bat were very sad. They didn't want to take him back but Emily could not fix the Bat from sleeping unside down. So they all walked the Bat back to the dream pet shop, so that they could all say goodbye.

Suddenly, The Bat began to fly around above Emily's head. He was trying to tell her something but she could not understand all his squeeking sounds. 'squeek, squeek' called the Bat. All the children looked at each other confused. 'What was he trying to say?' said May.

Then he began to fly away in a different direction. 'The Bat is flying away. All that sleeping upside down must have turned his head dizzy.' Shouted May. 'Come on everyone we need to catch him, come on.' called Emily.

The Bat flew high and low and led them to the town zoo, where he continued to fly inside. 'He's heading for the Zoo, FOLLOW THAT BAT !' shouted Emily. The children all followed him inside.

Emily and friends all ran into the zoo and search everywhere for the Bat. 'A tiny Bat could hide anywhere in such a big Zoo' exclaimed Emily worriedly. After a lot of searching they found him but they were very, very shocked at what they saw.

They saw a whole family of Bats in a cage and they were all **UPSIDE DOWN !!!** 'oh no ! his whole family is broken. This is worse than I thought ! What can we do ?' cried Emily. All the friends could not believe their eyes, as they had never seen something so silly in all their lives.

Suddenly, there is a loud laugh from behind her. 'Oh don't worry little girl, didn't you know that all Bats sleep upside down' Said Mr Paw the friendly zoo keeper. 'Bats love to hang upside down. They are not broken, they are very happy that way.' They were all very surprised to hear what Mr. Paw had to say, as he never everything about every animal.

The Bat flew in and hung on to Mr Paws finger. He did look very happy. 'You mean we didn't need to stand on our heads or glue furniture to the ceiling to make him happy' Thought Emily. Mr. Paw and the bat laughed at the thought. She did feel silly.

Mr Paw gave Emily a book all about Bats. It was full of interesting and amazing things that Bats can do. Everyone thought that Bats were wonderful creatures. Even Louie decided that he wanted to be a Bat when he grew up, so he could be in a scary movie or two. Mr Paw laughed.

They even saw a photo of a family of Bats all hanging upside down. They did look very happy.

'maybe I need to look at more books and learn about the amazing animal world more' said Emily.

Then Emily had an idea and she whispered it to all the friends. They all laughed but the Bat didn't know what the idea was.

'Today we all decided that we should try and see the world the way a bat sees it, UPSIDE DOWN, It can't hurt to see life the bats way !' exclaimed Emily. The Bat was very happy to see it and he really loved to have all his friends together with him.

Everyone laughed and enjoyed looking at the world upside down. Suddenly, Emily's toes began to loose grip. 'I think I know why Bats don't where shoes' she said in a worried voice.

Then Emily fell out of the tree, something a real Bat would never do.

Emily knew it was more difficult to be a Bat than she had first thought. She sat up with a dizzy head. 'Maybe we should put some glue on your feet' said Louie. The friends and the Bat laughed. They had learnt a lot about Bats today and I hope you did too.

'Bats are wonderful but maybe a bat is not the dream pet for me. What animal could I dream of next time.' Said Emily.

Can you guess which one she'll dream of next time ?

Little China

King Ra Ra

Odd Bod

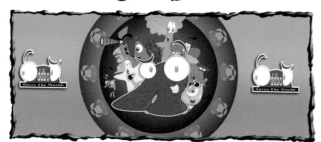

Mission - E

Flug and the Oddies

www.littlechina.cc

Printed in Poland
by Amazon Fulfillment
Poland Sp. z o.o., Wrocław